PAUL ZACHARIA

PAUL ZACHARIA

TWO NOVELLAS

PRAISE THE LORD
WHAT NEWS, PILATE?

translated by
GITA KRISHNANKUTTY

Published by

KATHA

A-3 Sarvodaya Enclave
Sri Aurobindo Marg, New Delhi 110017
Phone: 686 8193, 652 1752
Fax: 651 4373
E-mail: katha@vsnl.com
Internet address: http://www.katha.org

Published by Katha in February, 2001

KATHA is a registered nonprofit society devoted to enhancing the pleasures
of reading. KATHA VILASAM is its story research and resource centre.

This translation has been edited by Indira Chandrasekhar.

In-house Editors: Shoma Choudhury, Gita Rajan
Cover Design: Geeta Dharmarajan

Typeset in 9 on 15.5pt Bookman by Sandeep Kumar
at Katha and Printed at Pauls Press, New Delhi.

ISBN 81-87649-10-0

CONTENTS

PRAISE THE LORD 7

WHAT NEWS, PILATE? 49

PRAISE THE LORD

ANSY-WORK IN THE DAYTIME

This is what I like best, sitting here like this. I drag my easy
chair to the veranda and just sit, looking out at the courtyard.
The farm workers come and go. And once in a while, Ansy
calls out from the kitchen, asking me something or the other.
Tapioca, paddy and nutmegs dry on the mats spread across
the courtyard. I look beyond them and see pepper vines, coconut
palms, rubber and cocoa trees growing happily by themselves
without anyone asking them to do so. Fundraisers come by
once in a while. Sometimes the vicar drops in when he is out
for a walk. And occasionally relatives or friends drive in to
invite us to a wedding or some such event. I usually gulp

down a whiskey before lunch, which Ansy pours out and places on the table for me. And before my evening meal of chapatties, two more. These I take out myself from the bottle in the cupboard after my prayers. I stopped smoking long ago. Ansy can't bear the smell of tobacco.

And so I sit in the veranda, looking out. It rains and shines by turn. The hens run around. The children play. A cow breaks loose from its rope and wanders in. Or the two dogs have a game of You-Chase-Me-I-Chase-You. The flowering plants sway in the breeze. I feel content sitting here, watching all this, not having to go out anywhere.

In all these thirty five years I have not spent a single night in any other house if I could help it. Once evening sets in, I just have to get back to this home. As a boy I have sometimes slept over at my mother's taravadu. And I've spent an occasional half day at Ansy's house as well, to mark my presence at a wedding or funeral. But this veranda and this courtyard are really all I need.

The only time I go out is when I drop the children at school in the Mahindra. I've told them they must take the bus on their way back. Children so young shouldn't get used to travelling by car. I take out the Landmaster only on Sundays, to go to church. The very first car my father bought – so many years ago. To this day it doesn't have so much as a dent on it. You can hear the engine running only if you listen carefully.

The car is as old as I am. Yet I haven't heard it make a single unwanted rattle till now.

Early in the morning, I follow the rubber tappers into the estate on a quick round. After that, when the other workers have come in, I walk across to take a look at what they're doing. And once more later in the day, when the heat has cooled down. Once in a while I go to the rubber shed to watch the latex being pressed. That's all one needs to do. Everything can carry on by itself. All we have to do is lay down a system. There's no need at all to jump around and make a fuss. Do plants and trees and bulbs grow, do rubber trees give us sap, because they are frightened of us? They can do that by themselves. All we have to do is leave them to it.

But when I think of that one night last week, I get a jolt. Am I the same person who was there? It still feels like something that happened in another age. That doesn't mean I'm worried or anything. Oh no, what's there to worry about. Things like that don't happen all the time, even if we wanted them to. In a way, as I sit here looking at the shining sand in the courtyard, I feel like laughing, thinking back on all that confusion. Just this morning Ansy asked me, Joy, why are you sitting here laughing like this? Are you dreaming with your eyes wide open? It's nothing Ansy, I told her, I was just smiling at the glint of the sand in the yard. She came up to me at once and bent down to smell my face. Listening to you talk, I wonder if you've had a go at the bottle early in the morning without my knowledge, she said, sniffing at me. Ansy's face smells nicely of Cuticura talc. I stretched my hand out and squeezed her soft bottom. She fled to the kitchen. These, after all, are the pleasures of family life.

I have no desire to wander around the world or earn more wealth than I already have. Not at all. There is enough income from this property to marry off the one daughter I have. She's only ten now. And the younger boy is eight. This plantation, this house, all the blessings God has showered on me, who else are they for but the little fellow? I'd have no problems even if I had one or two more children. But Ansy seems to be unwilling. That's okay by me. If she doesn't want any more, there rests the matter. Coming to think of it, she's the one who has to carry them for ten months, bundle them up, rock them to sleep, nurse them, take care they don't hurt themselves, and bring them up painstakingly through sleepless nights. Let her tell me herself if she wants any more babies, right? I'm always ready. I'm always here, aren't I, sitting on this chair like this? She just has to say the word and I'll be ready.

When I look at our bed in the daytime, I often feel desire grow in me. And yet, in all these years, I've never been able to lay my hands on Ansy during the day, not one single time, despite trying every single trick. At night, though, there's never been a problem. Everything's okay. Only, she reminds me to take care, No babies. I sometimes ask her, Ansy, do you tell the priest at confession that you practise birth control? Oh, God knows all this, doesn't He, is her reply. How can I talk to the priest about such things? she asks. These women are made of better stuff than us in some matters. I have only seen Ansy as she is at night and it is always a bit shadowy. So I keep wondering what she'd look like in the daytime. But the way our house is, there's not a single room in it whose door is shut in the daytime. If you saw a closed door, you'd feel troubled. It's an open house.

The other day, having managed to send off the children to the cinema with the maidservant, I coaxed and lured Ansy into bed and had just about started enjoying the look of her when I heard someone cough in the courtyard. The carpenter's wife, our neighbour on the eastern side of our house, had arrived with her children to watch the Malayalam film on television. How could we not let them watch? Her husband is the only ashari who condescends to do odd jobs. These days, where can you find a carpenter who does that? But *my* work, my Ansy-work of daytime, that got cancelled!

THE ARRIVAL OF THE LOVERS

All I know about Delhi is from what I've read in the newspapers. I've read that it's both very cold and very hot there, and that Clinton and Gorbachev and such like visit there. Then I've seen the Republic Day parade and its dust raising displays on the television. I'm absolutely fed up with watching these. In spite of all these parades and things, the number of beggars coming to our house has only gone up, not come down. And when I see the arrogance of these Delhiwalas, I turn off the television and go out to sit in the veranda. Will the poor folk here get enough to eat just because these fellows shout and hoot in some alien language? But all this doesn't matter to

Ansy and the children. They watch it all.

Just think! A problem travels all the way from Delhi and creeps into this house of mine that lies at the other end of the country. It was our friend Sunny the lawyer who started it over the phone. Joy, there's a small problem, I need some help. Can I come over? he asked. Come, Sunny, come, I said. I'm just sitting here doing nothing. And I called out inside, Ansy, our vakil-saar is coming. Keep some coffee and snacks ready. Are there any more of those achappams your Ammachi sent the other day? So now there are takers for those achappams you found fault with then, are there? Ansy shouted back triumphantly. I take back what I said that day, I told her. Why argue unnecessarily with women? If you keep them happy, there's never any trouble.

Sunny arrived after a while. He speaks the measured language of a lawyer, but he's a good one. Only, he is slightly afflicted with the Kerala Congress bug. God knows how he caught it. I don't consider this a problem, though. After all, he and I have spent countless days together, diving and rowing and snatching favours from washerwomen on the wooded river bank!

Devaki's laughter those days had the sparkling sheen of the clothes she made white! All we had to do was catch her eye, and the sounds of her washing would not be heard for quite a while. Devaki always smelt of fine washing soap. One day, sitting on the leafy branches we had spread out behind the bushes for our session, she told Sunny smilingly, Sunny-cha, it was your mundu I was washing when you called me. Hey then, don't sit here, go back right away. That's the mundu I have to wear to a wedding tomorrow. Don't mess it up, Sunny said. Is it any wonder he went on to become a vakil?

He somehow landed himself in that Kerala Congress trap. Such a shame. You would never get me into it. However much Maani-saar might have achieved, I will not shift loyalty from the Congress that my father voted for. Never. When all is said and done, this Congress is a family tradition. And after all, there will always be good-for-nothing fellows in every good family.

Sunny parked his Maruti – this rotten Maruti is a car I can't bear to look at, it's no match, not even worth tying to the tail of an Ambassador on our roads – under the casuarina tree in the yard. He came in with a very serious expression on his face and sat down on a chair. No trace of his usual smile. Nor did he call out to Ansy to ask her how she is. What's up Sunny, I asked. Why so serious? Has your Kerala Congress split again? Or did one of your false witnesses let the cat out of the bag? Or have you caught AIDS? What's the matter? Lowering his voice he said, Joy, it's better that Ansy doesn't hear this. Let's go out into the yard and talk. I went with him past the fence, to where the nutmeg and cocoa stand.

Then Sunny says to me, Eda Joy, I might have to hide one,

maybe two, persons here. I froze. Good heavens, hide people in my house? What is he talking about? The only hiding I've seen is in my childhood – Ichachan hiding from fundraisers in the inner room. Then, hadn't we all read in the papers that Rajiv Gandhi's killers were hiding in Bangalore or some place like that? Is it a murderer he is asking me to hide? How is that possible in this house, where I live so happily with Ansy and the children? I stood staring at him for a while, unable to speak. Then I said, Eda Sunny, have you gone crazy? How can I hide murderers in my house with Ansy and the children here? Don't you know even that much about me? He gripped my shoulder and said, Am I such a fool, Joy? This is no murderer, it's a girl and a boy. What? A girl and a boy? Yes, they're lovers.

I fell for that. In all my life I'd never seen a pair of lovers face to face. I've seen them in the movies. But movies are not real. And I've read about them in novels. Those are not real either. But I knew for a fact that there is this tribe of people called lovers. Because there are always so many reports in the papers about lovers committing suicide. And so much more about them getting married in police stations! But I'd never seen such people in the flesh.

We once had a blacksmith girl and an ezhava boy living near us who were lovers. But I had never seen them together. The only time I did was when someone came running to say that they were hanging from one of the rubber trees in our eight acre plot on the western side. Pappi, the rubber tapper, had gone out there to tap at 4 am, wearing his headlamp. As he laid his knife on that tree, he felt something brush against his shoulder. He turned around in fright and saw them in the glow of the headlamp, the two of them, swaying, face to face. It was the girl's foot that had brushed his shoulder. He ran, screaming, jumped into the river and swam downstream. No one knows to this day where my three hundred rupee lamp has gone. Pappi was in bed with fever for a month. To this day, he gets tremors every now and then. I had that rubber tree cut down. Just think! It was a tree that gave me three coconut shells full of sap before eight every morning.

My question is, is it for this that people become lovers? How much better it is to be married, like me, to keep your wife in good humour, and to live a good life with children, than to rush into death in the cause of love. Let me tell you the truth, after I married Ansy, I've never flirted, not even with a grass cutting girl. I have stolen looks unwittingly at one or two women who worked in our kitchen. But when I thought of the look Ansy would give me in turn my looks cancelled them out.

Also, when we went to Goa to see the relics of St Francis Xavier, Sunny, I, Kuttichan and Tommy had downed three or four fenis and gone to the beach, giving our women the slip. Once we got there, there was nothing to do but to gape at the bottoms and breasts of those white women. But what use was that? What language would we speak in, to get close to them? Besides, the air is full of AIDS these days. So we hung around for a bit, then came back, bought two more bottles of feni, some good fried pork, and had a great time. When I woke up in the morning, Ansy said, You're shameless, Joy. Sorry, Ansy, I had one too many. That's something I've seen before. But what were you blabbering in your sleep? What? I asked. *Madamme, vaat is yuvar nayme, come hee-yar, I lowe you.* That's what you said, Joy. Lucky the children were asleep, Ansy said. I stood dazed as if I had been struck. Ansy, my own, I said, I had a nightmare, that I was very ill, lying in a hospital run by white women. I must have said *I giwe you,* not *I lowe you.* I was telling them not to worry, that I'd pay at once when they brought me the fat bill. Don't tell anyone about this, Ansy sweetheart, please. Don't bring shame on me.

Ansy tortured me no end and then finally struck a deal – silence in return for a stone-studded three sovereign necklace she had spotted in Mattathil Vakkachan's jewellery shop in Pala. That's how ten thousand odd rupees of mine went down the drain, for having gone to see the original form of a white woman.

A QUESTION OF THE SOUL

Eda Sunny, I said, If they are lovers, I'll have a go at it. I'd like to know what these creatures are like. Have you seen people like them before? It's the first time for me as well, Sunny said. Except, of course, I've seen you and Ansy. Forget that, I said. Ansy and I are a mere husband-wife couple living together as good mates. Let alone love, I don't even get to sit beside her on any given day. Aren't lovers always in an embrace, whether it be day or night? Sunny mused. What, in reality, is this thing called love? Isn't it for love that these two ran away from Delhi and all that? In that case, what is it you feel for Ansy and I for Kochurani? Oh, I don't know, I said. We're not fated to enjoy all this. We should have thought of it when we were younger. We should have thought of it when we stalked the grass cutting girls in the bushes near the stream. We should have fallen in love then. That's right, Sunny agreed. What's gone is gone, I said. Now quickly finish telling me about them. I need to know if there's any trouble involved because, you must realize, I can't hide them here without informing Ansy. I'll tell Ansy, he said, There's an angle to all this. Okay then, tell me quickly. I'll support you if there's no question of suicide or some such thing. It's not a question of suicide, said Sunny. It has to do with the soul.

The gist of what Sunny told me is as follows. The boy and the girl got to know each other in Delhi. She has a good job and so does he. The girl was born and brought up in Delhi but her father belongs to one of those crazy Christian sects. They used to be Catholics but somehow fell into strange ways. The boy comes from a first class family in Karimannur. Just his share of the property is a hefty twenty seven acre rubber plantation. The two met at one of those believers' gatherings in Delhi – at a Proclamation of the Divine Word-cum-Retreat. The boy was already a follower of this Charismatic business and used to go to their centre at Pottah even earlier. The girl's father – he too has a big job in Delhi – forced her to go to the Retreat because she had fallen into bad company in Delhi. Remember, she's one of those girls who's been around all of a big city like Delhi, walking in and out of restaurants, speaking English and Hindi and what not. Anyway, she obeyed her father and went to the Retreat. It so happened that the two of them were sitting next to each other there, singing and clapping. Maybe in Delhi they don't have separate enclosures for males and females, like we do here. Anyway, as happens during these Charismatic sessions, he placed his hands on her head and she did vice versa. And they were drawn to each other. And then, who knows, they must have gone to the cinema together, had coffee together in restaurants, sat together in parks, counted the stars, written letters to each other, and talked over the phone. In short, they became lovers.

So, did she get herself pregnant? I asked. Is that the problem? Eda Sunny, I'm not going to be party to an abortion, I don't feel good about that. Sunny smiled wickedly and asked, Then what was it for, that you gave three hundred and fifty rupees to Black Cat Kuttiamma, years ago? Do you remember? Quiet, I said. That was because she tricked me, she wasn't pregnant or anything. Don't give me that yarn, said Sunny. Okay, okay, now tell me what you want, I said.

It's not pregnancy that's the problem, Sunny said. I made enquiries. Someone sent the boy's family an anonymous letter and they got to know about the relationship. Those Karimannur people – an A-class family that we can say sprouted from the church wall itself in terms of ancestry – they won't just write off twenty seven acres of prime RRIM 105 grade rubber. And not just because the girl's family are part of a strange sect in god-forsaken Delhi, but also because the family lineage is not up to the mark. No pedigree at all and some caste problem on the mother's side as well – they come from a stock of low caste converts. But you wouldn't say any of this if you saw the girl. She's a smart little beauty.

Is that so, I asked. Yes, said Sunny. You wouldn't be able to take your eyes off her. You'd have to stick a label on her to convince people that she's the daughter of some wishy-washy Christian. Pink-cheeked, an oval face, hair cut very short almost like yours and mine. Ayyo! I said. But she's so pretty, said Sunny. Slim and willowy. Tall and shapely. You know those fashion models you see in the English magazines, she looks like them in jeans and shirt. Come off it, I said. You're kidding me. No, said Sunny, I swear by your father, it's true! I forgave him that father business. After all, it was to me he had come with his problem.

So what's the real problem, tell me, I said. I'll tell you, said Sunny. As soon as they got to know about the affair the boy's folks landed in Delhi overnight, to bring him back. But an autorickshaw driver took them for a ride and they got lost. Finally, they had to make a call to the boy at his office. I'm just coming, he told them, and instead, rushed home, packed some clothes and money, picked up the girl from her office, and vanished. Didn't the girl have to take her clothes? I asked. Eda, said Sunny, If you have money on you, are clothes a problem? Aren't the shops full of them? In any case, I said, Maybe lovers don't need too many clothes. I don't know about that, said Sunny. Anyway, what the boy says is that the previous day, while he was meditating, the Holy Spirit had informed him that his folks were coming to get him. Not bad! I said.

Sunny continued, By the time his family discovered what had happened, the two of them had vanished without a trace. And all this, imagine, in the land of the Hindi speaking people. However, his folks have political clout. And they're a damned proud lot. They squandered money on a hotel room and stayed on – they met MPs and the police and told them the boy had been kidnapped – they filed a criminal petition against the girl's family. The foolish cultists fell on their knees, praying and wailing for mercy. But would the Karimannur folk relent at any of this? No chance! They extracted the information from her parents that the girl had telephoned to say she was going to Kerala. They rushed back here at once. And they got the Kerala police moving with calls from Delhi.

Where were the lovers during all this? I asked. In a star hotel in Kochi. A star hotel? I asked. Yes. Have you forgotten the fact that it's in a twenty seven acre estate that the boy has his RRIM 105 grade rubber? But for your stinginess, you too could stay in a star hotel as long as you liked, said Sunny. Oh, come off it, I said. A mat and a pillow at home are all I need. Did they stay together at the hotel, Sunny? No, he said sarcastically, Separately, isn't that what they ran away for? That's not what I mean Sunny, I said. A boy who is blessed by the Holy Spirit alone with a girl ... That's what's special about being Charismatic, Sunny said. He didn't touch even a hair on her head. I found out by asking both of them. Oh, I see, so these are the things you find out on the strength of being a lawyer? Shouldn't I know these things in the event of something going wrong with the case? Sunny said. Try that on someone else, I said. Don't I know you? Enough of joking around, said Sunny, The matter is serious. In Delhi the girl's family is being taken to the police station every other day and intimidated. Whenever she calls them, they weep and wail over the phone. And the boy and the girl tell them, Don't be afraid, Daddy and Mummy, we're praying for you every day, that's that.

The Kerala police located the hotel they had been staying in, in Kochi. But when they knocked on the door, the couple had left for Pottah. The police went to the Retreat Centre in Pottah in civilian clothes. They couldn't find the lovers amidst the clamour and confusion of the prayer meeting. But the Lord pointed out the police to them – at least that's what the boy says. *Praise the Lord!* I said. That's all right, said Sunny, Now listen to the rest of the story without showing off. The lovers got away from Pottah in a taxi. And early this morning when I went out to the veranda on hearing the dog bark, there they were, standing in my courtyard.

How is that possible? What connection do they have with you? Are you such a famous lawyer, I asked, to needle him. That's where the problem lies, said Sunny. The girl's paternal uncle is a big gun in the Kerala Secretariat. He's on their side. And my application for appointment as Public Prosecutor is lying on his table. I've been to see him many times. I believe he told the boy on the phone, You only have to go to Palai and meet Sunny vakil, he'll do everything for you. Oh, so you've hit the jackpot, I said. If you sort this out, you're a Public Prosecutor. I can't be sure of that, said Sunny, But how can I not help them out? At the same time, I can't keep them at home. If the police should turn up, there goes my chance of becoming the Public Prosecutor! Also, I don't trust Kochurani's loose tongue one bit. What I've told her is that they're friends of our Bombay Georgekutty and that they've just stopped by on their way to the Retreat at Pottah. Fortunately for me, they've been singing and praying ever since they arrived. The girl can't speak Malayalam, but if the Spirit possesses the boy all of a sudden and he blurts the truth to Kochurani, it will be a total mess.

Eda Sunny, I said, I'm just a dunderhead farmer, but may I suggest a solution? Tell me, said Sunny. Take them quickly to a registry office, get them married, and then present them before

Inspector Balachandran-saar. He's our man, isn't he? Just have a word with him in advance and there won't be a problem. But that's where the biggest problem lies, said Sunny. The boy is absolutely against a registered marriage. He wants to get married in Pottah, singing and praying, directly under the gaze of the Holy Spirit. He says this is a matter that concerns his soul. A matter of his soul for him and a matter of your job for you, I said. Which is more important? Sunny remained silent.

After a while Sunny said, The boy is a moron too, he says that if he falls into the hands of his father and older brothers, he won't be able to go against them. So he's praying for a change of heart to come over them. I asked him secretly, Samkutty, are you saying you'll abandon this girl if you fall into the hands of your father and brothers? Abandon is only a word, Chetta, he tells me, A word that we have invented. If I surrender to my father and brothers, it will be because God wills it. If Annie has to part ways with me and go away, that too will be God's will. No one abandons anyone, Chetta, it is God who does everything. That poor girl, I said to Sunny.

There's something funny about her too, Sunny said. She doesn't believe in marriage, that's what she told me. In Jawaharlal Nehru University, where she studied, no one believes in marriage. She says she likes Samkutty's singing, his gentle nature and his humility. And she's done meditation and all that in Rajneesh's ashram in Pune and she likes it. She enjoys going to the disco. She says that for her this trip is spiritual net-surfing. If the girl says she doesn't believe in marriage, what will you do now? I asked Samkutty. His reply to me is that he's praying for her and that a change of heart will come over her when she goes to the Retreat at Pottah. And then she too says, Chetta, I'm keeping my heart open so that God can make it change. At which Samkutty springs up, cries out *Praise the Lord*, links hands with her and begins to dance with eyes shut. This is what happened.

This really is a problem, Sunny, I said. What will you do? Let them stay here for a couple of days, Sunny said. You and Ansy can try talking to them. I'll try and handle the police meanwhile and see if I can get these two to Pottah. By then, you and Ansy must somehow get the girl to believe in marriage.

What'll we tell Ansy? I asked. Let me handle that. I'll tell her the plain truth, said Sunny. Women are like us, they too have seen lovers only in films, I'm pretty sure. And there are two of them walking straight into the house. I'll get Ansy to agree. There's just one problem, you'll have to see to that. Tell me, I said. The Karimannur people have sent out Kulappuram Vakkan and two other rowdies in search of these two. So you'll have to be careful. Oh Yeshu, I said, This is indeed a serious problem, Sunny. He went into the kitchen looking for Ansy without a word in reply.

AN INVITATION TO FIREFLIES

I don't think they'll come now, Ansy said when she heard the clock strike ten. Having said our prayers and put the children to bed, we were sitting on the ledge in the lower veranda waiting for Sunny to arrive with the lovers. There were fireflies on all the plants in the yard. The light of a half moon lay on the sand, but the moon could not be seen at all.

No, they're sure to come, I said. We'll wait a little longer and then go to bed, said Ansy. Who shall we say they are, to the kids tomorrow? I asked. We'll tell them they are friends of our Mathachan in Delhi and that they've come to see Kerala, she said. Then we must tell the lovers to stick to the same story, I said. Otherwise we'll say one thing, the lovers another and the kids will blow the whistle. Children these days ...

Well, Ansy said, The problem is they're your children, aren't they? So the responsibility is all mine now, is it? Then why do you tempt me all the time with all those soft things of yours, I said, and caught Ansy in a tight hug. Do you know something, I whispered in her ear. All these fireflies are flashing their light because they're lovers. They're calling out to each other. Shh ... We're out in the veranda, Joy, she said, rolling away from me along the veranda. It's our very own veranda after all, Ansy, my little darling, let's be lovers for a bit, I said. I had just pulled her towards me catching hold of her foot and begun to tickle her sole when the headlights of a car turned in at the gate. Shh, didn't I tell you, Joy, Ansy said and, giving me a kick, she scrambled up, went into the house and shut the door behind her.

By the time I went down to the yard with the torch Sunny's Maruti had come to a halt. He got out of the car and came up to me. The back door opened and Samkutty got out. He had a gentle face and smile and wore a long sleeved white shirt and white trousers. He looks like a cute little seminarian all right, I thought to myself. He bent down towards the car and said in English, Come, Annie. And I told myself, Oh, it's all in English. How am I going to advise her then? Annie slid along the seat and put both her legs out. Legs that shone like alabaster in the moonlight. She was wearing a black skirt that came below her knees and a short black and white shirt. Something white glittered on her feet. I looked closer – silver anklets. She sat there in the car and smiled. Then she got out and waited near the car with arms crossed. Joy, this is Annie and this is Samkutty, Sunny said. Annie smiled, Hullo, Uncle. Then she patted her short hair and pushed back the wisps that had fallen on her forehead. What Sunny had said is true, I thought. A lovely oval face, a give-and-take body. Her teeth gleamed when she smiled. Her legs glistened like butter. I examined both their faces closely. Is there anything special about them? Anything peculiar to lovers?

At first sight, I didn't notice anything. Sunny took their things out of the car and put them on the veranda. By that time Ansy was back, standing in the veranda. I said to Samkutty and Annie, Come in, have a bath if you want to, and then we can eat. Ansy, take them inside. When they had gone into the house, I said to Sunny, So, that's how it is. Yes, said Sunny. Just be patient for a day or two. I'll organize everything by then. Eda Sunny, I said, That's your problem. But what about mine, if Kulappuram Vakkan comes? Please manage somehow, said Sunny. Where's that double barrelled gun that your father had? I don't even know how to load bullets in it, I said. You don't need bullets, Sunny said. All you need to do is to take it out and point it.

Any rowdy will run away. Let me see, I said.

Ansy was talking to them when I went in. Samkutty and Annie were seated close to each other on the sofa. Samkutty was saying to Ansy, Chechi, forgive us for bothering you like this. Don't think of us only as lovers. We are also on a pilgrimage in search of God. Aren't we, Annie? Annie nodded and smiled, displaying all thirty two of her jasmine like teeth. Where have you been, besides Pottah? asked Ansy. We didn't go anywhere else, said Samkutty. This is a pilgrimage of the heart, Chechi. Ansy smiled, looked at Annie and asked, When is your wedding going to be? You mustn't forget to invite us. Annie said something to Samkutty in English, and he in turn said, Annie says we'll go to Pottah and get married as and when God wills it. After all that you have gone through, won't it be a waste if you don't get married now? Ansy asked. He asked Annie something in English. Then he said to Ansy, Annie says our love cannot be limited by marriage. Annie said something again and Samkutty repeated promptly, Chechi, we are but refugees of love. These wanderings of ours are a brave journey of the soul, a spiritual adventure, isn't that so, Annie? But don't let that muck up poor Sunny's Public Prosecutor job, oh lovers, I said to myself.

Annie smiled broadly again, displaying her jasmine buds, and nodded her agreement to Samkutty. Then she stretched out both her legs, slid her slippers to the ground and stroked one leg with the foot of the other. I watched from the corner of my eye. Each of her toes was like a rosebud. When I noticed Ansy gesturing to me from the inner room, I thought she had caught me looking. But actually she was calling to speak to me in confidence.

How shall we arrange for them to sleep? Do we put them in the same room? Ansy asked. I stood as if I'd been struck by lighting. Oh Lord, that's true. I hadn't given that any thought. You have a point, Ansy, what do you think? I assumed you would have thought about it, she said. It didn't occur to me, I said. Shall we phone Sunny and ask? No, said Ansy, They'll hear us. In that case, we'll give them separate places, I said. Let him sleep in the enclosed veranda and she in the room that Ammachi used to sleep in. But, said Ansy. But what? I asked. Ansy poked me with a finger and said, What if they get up in the night and sleep together? Would it be proper to lock the room? I asked. Look, there's one thing. Didn't Sunny tell us that so far they haven't touched even a hair on each other. Then why are we worrying so much? Ansy said. We'll put them in the same room, let them do what they want. After all we're not going to decide on their sleeping arrangements in the future. That's right, I said. If they want to touch each other, let them do it in our house, yes? I pinched Ansy's warm thigh and said, Hey, maybe they too will feel like doing something when they see what those fireflies are up to. Then Ansy turned serious,

Didn't the girl say that she was reluctant to get married? Maybe she'll change her mind when she's here. We'll let them sleep together, that's the way it should be. Yes, I said.

Ansy and I put the two beds side by side in the enclosed veranda, spread freshly washed and ironed sheets over them, kept a clean blanket on top, changed the pillowcases and placed two glasses of milk and a bottle of water on the table. And fresh towels and soap in the bathroom. When we went back they were both standing in the yard, looking at the moon. Not bad, I thought to myself, that's more like lovers. Standing in the veranda, I cleared my throat and said, Shall we all go to bed then? I took them to the enclosed veranda where Ansy was shutting the windows. Samkutty protested, Ayyo, please don't shut them, Chechi. Annie says we should leave the doors and windows open to invite the fireflies in. Samkutty and Annie laughed. You have fine desires, my girl, I said to myself. With those alabaster legs of yours, you have no eyes for the decent human beings here, but you want those useless fireflies. I said to Samkutty, Since you are, in a manner of speaking, in hiding, it's better that you keep the windows and doors closed. God will look after us, Joy Chetta, Samkutty said, looking up at the sky. The same God who's looking after your poor father and mother and also Kulappuram Vakkan, I said to myself.

Before going to bed, I took Ichachan's gun out from behind the pathayam and leaned it against the wall, near my cot.

Ansy rolled her eyes when she saw it and looked at me. It's to protect the lovers, and if you give me a tight hug, I'll be braver still, I said, making my way close to Ansy. I'm so sleepy, I can't do a thing, she said. Think of what they must be doing now, I said. Do you think everyone is crazy like you? They must be fast asleep, snoring. Ansy released herself from my embrace as she said this, and lay down facing the wall. Go to sleep, Joy, she said.

I lay in the dark with my eyes open. A thousand thoughts passed through my mind. What is that girl like, I wondered. She'll melt like butter wherever she is touched, I'm sure. Oh Lord, two lovers who had come from god knows where, were asleep in my house. Something of their love will be left here even after they go. Refugees of love. Are there really people like that? After some time, I couldn't bear it any longer. I got up quietly, walked out to the veranda, and going across to its enclosed part, peeped in, hiding behind a pillar. Ansy was right. They were lying on the cot, back to back, fast asleep, with the windows and doors open. I came back, stood for a while looking at Ansy, then got into bed and covered myself completely. I felt as if overcome by sudden terror.

REAL COURAGE

I woke up with a start hearing the roar of a motorcycle. I sat up, shaking, and said to Ansy, who was awake, Go and lie down with the children. Let me go and see who that is.

Don't go out to the veranda, Joy, said Ansy. I picked up the gun, peered through the shutters of the window and asked, Who is it? It's me, Joy Chetta, Jose, Sunny's younger brother, said the person on the motorcycle. Well, what brings you here at this time, Jose, I said, putting the gun down and going out to the veranda. Jose said, Chettan sent me to tell you that there is a suspicion that Vakkan and gang are coming this way. He said you must be careful, Joy Chetta, and that you'd better hide the Delhiites well. Chettan sent me here and has gone to the Inspector's house himself. He asked me to keep you company here. Come into the house, Jose, I said. Don't stand there in the yard. The clock struck two. My legs were shaking as I walked in to look for Ansy. My body felt limp. I had trembled like this only once long ago, when the elephant that was brought to carry timber at Madukkakunnu had gone berserk and rushed at me. Eda Joy, I said to myself, There's nothing to tremble about. It's Ichachan's gun you have in your hand.

I took Ansy aside without waking the children and explained the situation to her. If you're so worried, why did you get into this? she said. Is Kulappuram Vakkan going to come here to kill and eat all of us? Is this a place where anyone can get away with doing whatever they want? We live here as well, don't we? What you say is true, I said. But what if they grab those two sleeping there and take them away, won't we lose face? The boy will be beaten up and what about the girl? And what will I tell Sunny? Isn't this prosecutor job a long standing desire of his? So we have to do something. Ansy said, We'll hide them in the attic of that coconut store for now. The coconuts were taken down the day before yesterday and the attic has been swept and cleaned. But the carpenter's removed the ladder for repair. That doesn't matter, I said, We can use a table and a stool on top of it, for them to climb up.

Jose sat in the veranda and smoked a cigarette. Go and wake them up, Ansy said to me, Jose and I will bring the table. I went to the side of the enclosed veranda and peered in through the window. They were fast asleep, covered to the neck. The girl was curled up like the letter S. I called out Samkutty's name twice and he jumped up. I said to him, Samkutty, the Karimannur people have sent Kulappuram Vakkan here to take you away. We have to be prepared for your father and brothers to be with them as well. Sunny has asked me to hide you well. The best place to hide here is the attic of the coconut store. You'll have to be careful not to bump your heads on the ceiling, that's all. Just for a short while. Once they're gone, you can come down. We'll give you mats and pillows, you can lie down there and go to sleep. Are my father and brothers coming, Chetta? asked Samkutty. They're likely to, I said. Would he send a rowdy by himself to catch hold of his son? Samkutty looked heavenward suddenly and prayed, Our Father who art in Heaven, please show me the light in the matter of this chalice that I carry. I felt like bashing his chin in for calling the lamb like girl *this chalice*. At this rate, Samkutty, I told him silently, You're going to have one hell of a time drinking from that chalice. Wake Annie up quickly, I said aloud. We should move to the coconut store.

He shook Annie and she jumped up and sat on the cot, staring at us. For a while I couldn't breathe. Amma! All she was wearing was a little dress made of something like a polythene sheet, that showed everything. What a sight it was, even though there was not much light in the room. I wanted to flash the torch in my hand all over her. I wondered if anyone could hear the thumping of my heart – *dhum, dhum*. While Samkutty was telling her what had happened, you wouldn't believe this, she walked across and turned on the light herself. I looked at her quickly. She was standing there casually, listening to what Samkutty was saying. And there I was, looking at him, looking at her, looking everywhere. My hands shook. Let Ansy not come in now, I prayed. When I could bear no more of it, I went over and turned off the light and said, Let's not keep the light on, it will lead to problems. My voice sounded like someone else's.

As soon as Samkutty stopped explaining the situation to her, she clapped her hands, jumped up and down, making everything that was beneath the see through robe shake, and did a little dance, singing a song in English. Samkutty explained, Annie is praising the Lord, Chetta, saying that we are now performing really courageous deeds. *Praise the Lord*, I responded. Annie says this experience is as thrilling as something she has seen in the movies. She thanks you too, for giving her such an opportunity. *Praise the Lord*, I said, *No mention, no mention*. It was only when she picked up a sheet and wrapped it around her like a mundu that I was able to breathe again.

When I reached the coconut store with the two of them, Ansy and Jose were about to go and fetch the mats and pillows. I sent Samkutty up first, helping him climb the table and then the stool. Pull Annie up and help her, Samkutty, I said. Annie, still clad in the sheet, climbed on to the table and balanced herself carefully on the stool. But she couldn't hoist herself any higher. Samkutty gripped her hand but couldn't lift her up. Chetta, can you help her up? he asked.

In a flash I am on the table, lifting her by the waist. Perhaps because Samkutty's grip is not tight enough, she keeps sliding down. I push her up, holding her buttocks in my palms, and she slides down further letting out a funny laugh, and the sheet she is wrapped in comes undone and falls over my head. I can't see a thing. My God, let Ansy not come now, I pray silently, and gathering her up in my arms, I climb up on the stool and hand her up to the attic. I take the sheet off my face and give it to her. Sorry, she says, looking at me. *No problem*, I say, *Not at all problem*. And I sit down on the table gasping for breath, as if I had just run away from some great danger. I cannot speak because her odour is in my nostrils, her softness in my chest and the feel of her body in the palms of my hand.

Just then, Ansy and Jose came in. Don't stir from there unless Ansy or Jose or I call you, I shouted up to the attic. No, Chetta, it was she who answered. And then, like before, there was the sound of her laughter. Laugh, girl, laugh, I said to myself, This is laughing time for you.

Give me a mat, Chechi, I'll sleep in the veranda, Jose said. As Ansy went in to get the mat, two jeeps came in one after the other through the gate. They had no lights. This is it, Jose, I said. Turning on the light outside, Jose and I stepped into the yard. Jose whispered, Yes, it's them. I remembered that I'd left the gun near the cot. A thin tall man with a bath towel tied around his head as headgear and protruding veins stepped out of the first jeep. He wore a transparent white jubba and a gold chain and had a thin handlebar moustache. His mundu was tucked high over his stomach. He was swaying slightly. It's Kulappuram Vakkan himself – in flesh and blood – I thought to myself. I had seen him only once before, at the annual Jubilee Festival of our parish church. Three or four men clad in lungies and banians got out of the jeep after him. A fair, fat, bald old man and two or three youngsters got down from the other jeep. The old man wound the thin veshti that lay on his shoulder around his neck. The young men had Samkutty's Older Brothers written all over them.

We looked at them and they looked at us. Behind me, I heard Ansy come out onto the veranda. Why did she have to come out, I thought. Couldn't she have stayed inside with the children? Vakkan lit a beedi, pulled at it once and turned and looked at the old man behind him. The old man came forward at once and asked, Isn't this the Mullathazhathu House? Yes,

I said. Is your name Joy? Yes, I said again. What is it you want at this time of the night? I asked. I did not, of course, show how frightened I was. I have information that my younger son Samkutty has been kidnapped and is being kept here in hiding. We've come to take him, said the old man. This is a real surprise! I said. Why should I kidnap your son? I don't even know who you are. Where are you people from? I'm Karimannur Kaduvakunnel Kunhukutty and these are my sons, said Samkutty's father. And all these people? I gestured with my head towards Vakkan and company. My friends, said the old man. We don't know who this is, said Vakkan, pointing his beedi at Jose. My younger brother, I said.

Out of the corner of my eye, I saw that Ansy had come down the steps and was standing by my side. My terror now shifted to the coconut store. What if that idiot heard his father's voice, came down, and wailed and begged for forgiveness? It would be all over for me, wouldn't it? I was more afraid of Samkutty sitting up there in the attic than of Kulappuram Vakkan. My safety depends on the girl's brightness, I said to myself.

You have a nerve, to come at the dead of night to a house where women and children are asleep and accuse us of kidnapping your son! Ansy said. I looked at Ansy. She was looking straight at the old man's face. I didn't say you kidnapped him, the old man said. My son and a girl were found missing in Delhi. We have information that they are hiding here, that's all I said. Vakkan lit another beedi, blew out the smoke, waved the matchstick slowly from side to side till it went out and said, to no one in particular, It will be good for all concerned if you let our boy out quickly. He flicked the burnt matchstick towards the house with one finger. Ansy marched right up to the old man.

As he stared at her, she pointed the index finger of her right hand at him, almost touching his face, and said, Come into our house and carry out a search, Chetta, if you have the guts. If your son is not here, you will not easily forget having entered this house for the rest of your life, or my father's name is not Chullikkamattathil Chandykunhu. The old man's face grew pale. John Chullikkamattam, the District Collector, was Ansy's father's younger brother's son. It was a fifty acre rubber estate at Vilakkumadam that he got as dowry, worth a crore and a half! The old man's face went white. It was because we had a well-founded suspicion that we ... he said. Ansy walked back, stood on the steps and waved her hands inviting him to enter. Come in, Chetta, clear your suspicion and then leave. Don't wake the children, that's all.

Vakkan twirled his moustache once, turned and looked at the old man and his sons. The sons murmured something to the old man. The old man got into the jeep and it drove off. Vakkan gave Jose and me one last piercing look and got into the other jeep. That drove off too. I stamped out the glowing beedi stub he had left in the courtyard. Ansy sat down on the lower veranda, stretched her legs out towards the steps, and smiled. Jose and I stood there looking at her. Then she said, Joy, my tongue is better than your non-performing gun. Jose laughed out loudly. I didn't say anything.

Let's see what state the lovers are in, I said. I went to the coconut store and called softly, Samkutty. I could hear sobbing sounds. I pulled up the table, stood on it, and flashed the torch. It's me, Joy, I said. Your father and the others have left, don't worry. Samkutty was sitting on the mat, sobbing away. The girl was by his side. She said to me, in a mixture of Malayalam and English, When Samkutty's *father* came, Samkutty's *mouth* I *closed* with my *hands*. Thank you, I said. Don't mention it, Chetta, she said. I turned off the torch and climbed down.

We didn't sleep after that. Ansy made us black coffee. It must have been around four in the morning, the cock had not crowed yet, when Sunny's Maruti drove in slowly and stopped in the yard. He didn't turn off the engine. Where are they? he asked. In the coconut store, I said. Shall I call them? Quickly, he said. We have to get to Vagamon before sunrise. Why Vagamon? Isn't it to Pottah you have to go? I asked. Going to Pottah will be a problem. There's a Retreat going on at Vagamon. I've spoken to the priest there and fixed everything. The marriage can still be conducted in the holy spirit pervailing at the Retreat, he said.

Full of happiness, I walked towards the coconut store. As I got up on the table, I felt a thrill run through my body. I said, Sunny has come to take you, you can come down now. It was the girl who came down first. She descended into my outstretched arms like a flying angel. Keeping her standing on the table, I climbed down to the ground, lifted her once again and put her down. She wore the sheet around her waist like a mundu. By the time I stretched my hands for Samkutty, he had come down by himself. After that, without much delay, Annie in her black skirt and black and white top, and Samkutty in his white long sleeved shirt and white trousers, got into Sunny's car and left. Ansy watched them leave with her hand on her chin and said, Poor things, how much they have to suffer just so that they can love each other a little!

PRAISE THE LORD

As I said, I am sitting in this veranda once again, doing nothing. Once in a while, Ansy calls out from the kitchen, asking me something or the other. Tapioca, paddy and nutmeg dry on the mats spread across the courtyard. I look beyond them and see pepper vines, coconut palms, rubber and cocoa trees, all growing happily by themselves, without anyone asking them to do so.

Sunny had visited suddenly, once, to tell us about what happened to those two. Even after two days of Retreat, the girl did not receive any indication of God's will. She invited Samkutty to establish a spiritually adventurous, unmarried family But Samkutty took her to Kochi in a taxi, and sent her off in a plane to Delhi. Sunny said Samkutty cried all the way, from Vagamon to Kochi and Kochi to Karimannur. On reaching home he ran to the prayer room and fell on his knees, wailing loudly. When they saw him, his father and his older brothers too wept loudly.

Sunny had accompanied them to Vagamon and participated in the Retreat for two days. So it's him I'm worried about now. As for his prosecutor papers, they're getting readied in Thiruvananthapuram. *Praise the Lord.*

Ansy was saying yesterday, why not propose our Maryamma Elemma's Janice for Samkutty? I remembered the twenty seven acres of RRIM 105 rubber and instantly agreed. Yes, we'll do that. *Praise the Lord.*

WHAT NEWS, PILATE?

PREFACE

THE YAKSHI OF PANCHAVANKADU

"Long ago, there was a woman who lived near Nagerkoil. She was young and had some riches of her own. She lived alone, with no men, nobody, to help her. One day a Tamil brahmin came to the place. He wooed the woman and had an affair with her. In three or four months, she became pregnant. When she was six months gone, the brahmin told her she should go and stay in Padmanabhapuram until her delivery. She trusted him, so she sorted out her worldly goods, sold everything and in the seventh month of her pregnancy, set out with the brahmin, carrying with her the money she had made and a bundle containing all her worldly possessions. They reached

Panchavankadu forest on a Friday afternoon. She soon grew tired walking over the stones in the forest, and could not manage another step forward. The brahmin asked her to sit down under a thorny cactus on the wayside and he too sat down beside her. She put her bundle down, opened it and gave the brahmin betel leaves to chew. He put his arms around her happily and drew her down on his lap. She fell asleep from sheer fatigue. The brahmin examined her face closely to make sure she was asleep, lifted her head slowly, placed it on a stone, and then hit it with another big stone. Her eyes flew open in pain, and seeing the brahmin standing over her, aiming the stone at her again, she pointed at the thorny cactus and shouted, Cactus, you are my witness! She slipped into the next world, gazing fixedly at the demon's face. As for the brahmin, he stole the bundle and all the jewels she was wearing, and calmly proceeded to Padmanabhapuram, where he lived in comfort."

Although Parukutty paid no attention to the story at first and sat thinking of other things, the mention of a woman, a husband, and particularly Panchavankadu, lured her into listening. Somewhat dissatisfied with hearing that the brahmin went to Padmanabhapuram and lived there happily, she said, "What a terrible thing! How cruel that brahmin was! He killed the woman who trusted him. When I think of such wicked men living happily in this world without having to face any suffering,

I am tempted to believe that such a thing as divine wrath does not exist."

Karthiyayani Amma: "Wait, daughter, how can you offer an opinion without having heard the story in full? The brahmin did get the punishment he deserved. One may not obtain just reward for one's actions in this world. But you cannot therefore come to the conclusion that this is an unjust world." And she continued the story, with renewed enthusiasm.

"The brahmin was punished without much delay. He had stopped travelling along that forest route until one day, friends invited him to go with them to the chariot festival in the temple at Suchindram. The brahmin at first said he was not interested in festivals, but the others would not accept any excuses and insisted on taking him along. When they came to Panchavankadu, they saw a very beautiful woman sitting under a banyan tree with a child who shone with a divine radiance seated in front of her. The woman kept looking at the travellers and making signs. She looked as if she was bathed in gold! She wore a saree of glittering silk. As for the tilakam on her forehead, the kajal in her eyes and her hairstyle, they were beyond description. And the fragrance of the flowers she wore!

"Realizing, from all these signs, that she was a prostitute, the travellers walked on, paying her no attention. But the brahmin could not resist turning around. He walked up to her slowly. It was a Friday afternoon. The brahmin and the woman started walking side by side. The things they did! Both of them forgot that the woman had a child with her. It is creatures like her who ruin a woman's reputation. The brahmin was intoxicated, overwhelmed by the flash of her eyebrows, the darting of her kajal rimmed eyes, her coy words, the little snatches of song she broke into, the gait that swayed her entire body, the tweaks and blows and pokes she gave his cheeks and chin. But why blame only women? If there were no men like this brahmin to dance to their tunes, would not women be a little more modest?

"Anyway, she led the brahmin to that same thorny cactus and sat him down at its foot. She took out betel leaves just as she had done long ago. The brahmin had forgotten all that had happened in the past. Is there anything on this earth as hard as the heart of men? Men who entice women with sweet nothings – My golden one, My dearest one, My silver one, and so on – are not to be trusted, not even in one's wildest dreams. Most of the time, only women possess that kind of heart melting affection. The two stones that the brahmin had once used lay near him. Ah, but he saw nothing. He was lost in the smile of the prostitute. He moved close to her and opened his mouth to take betel leaves from her mouth into his own. Suddenly screaming Ayyo, abba, she's cheated me, in a voice loud enough to shatter the entire Panchavankadu, the brahmin sprang up and began to run. He tripped over the very stone he had used long ago and fell down. The woman had dropped her guise and transformed herself into his pregnant wife. As he looked at her helplessly from where he had fallen, his wife's form too began to change. The Panchavankadu Yakshi herself stood before the brahmin, her figure rising as high as the sky and filling the forest – fearful, protruding teeth, a blood red tongue that reached the ground, a cavernous mouth, round eyes that scattered sparks of fire, and thick hair that stood erect like trees. Fire, smoke and roars of laughter poured out of the yakshi's mouth and nose and eyes. Oh Padmanabha! The poor brahmin ...

"My dear, why are you trembling? Are you frightened? After all, the story is almost over now, once I've said that the yakshi tore the brahmin in two, drank his blood and ate him up. That child was an illusion, created from a twig of the cactus. With the child as witness, the yakshi punished the brahmin in full measure for his crime. It is thus that we pay the price for our actions, some day."

C V Raman Pillai: *Marthanda Varma*, Chapter 3

WHAT NEWS, PILATE?

PONTIUS PILATE WRITES A LETTER

By the grace of Jupiter, the Father of the Universe; by the mercy of the Emperor of Rome, Tiberius Claudius Nero the unconquerable and beloved of his subjects; and under the signature and seal of Pontius Pilate, representative of the peerless Roman Empire and Governor of the entire province of Judaea.

Edo. Antonius!

Don't be amazed at the strange and wonderful titles above and the glorious colours of my seal. I know you are not the sort to be easily surprised. You must have known of my present situation when you finally decided to write to me. Suffice it to say that the Emperor, history and the divine Jupiter – I too have learned to chant Jupiter's name – have led me to where I am.

During the last quarter century, as I wandered around the world serving two Emperors, I often wondered where you were, what you were doing. But, despite using all the powers of investigation that the Roman Empire has, I couldn't spot even a bubble where you had sunk away. And then suddenly, like a flash of Jupiter's lightning (ha, there comes Jupiter again!) your letter arrives! It made me very happy, Antonius. I had begun to feel lonely and sad, as if life was turning dark, and it was then that my close friend from those good times chose to remember me. My thanks to you, friend. You know I am not usually given to showing emotion. Well, I have a lot to tell you, after all these years.

It is Sabbath today. So the Jewess who is my secretary is off. Are you smiling as you hear me say *secretary*? No, it's not what you think. It is true that she is beautiful. She knows Latin, Greek and Hebrew. I love her like my daughter. Aren't relationships of that sort too part of life? Ruth is such a nice name, isn't it? Why don't our Roman girls have such exciting names? Ruth is the daughter of one of the handmaids of my wife Julia. Now that she is not here, let me write you a few things in my own hand, without having to hide anything. In any case, shouldn't I use my own hand when writing to you?

Remember the times we were caned at school because of our handwriting?

Antonius, do you remember when we last parted? Twenty five years ago! We staggered down the steps of that dream like brothel south of the Coliseum, and dragged ourselves through the darkness, dust and blood on our bodies. What a day it was! When you tired of Turkish beauties and Macedonian boys, you demanded eunuchs. They brought us Egyptian ones. But they didn't smell good. So we flung the crockery around, insisting that they bring us Arabs. We smashed the bottles and overturned the tables. We pulled out our swords on the madam. I still remember how you shouted at her, pointing to me: It is a Deputy Commander of the Roman army who stands here! Take care! We'll be satisfied with nothing less than perfumed Arabs. Where have you hidden them? To please which senator? I stood behind you and weakly brandished my sword, but it slipped and fell to the ground. The young madam – who, even before she came to Rome, had fully imbibed the hardness of the Corsican mountains where she had been born – bared her opium stained teeth like a snake's fangs and smiled. She picked up the sword and shoved it back into the sheath at my waist. Then, tapping her index finger with its long nail on your chest and mine, she said (ah, the heat and odour of those moments!): You dogs! The mighty Roman Emperor himself is satisfied with the flesh I provide him. He has never complained.

And now – you two, a deputy commander and his crony! Put the money down and get out, you wretched shit! She lifted her black robe and mockingly bared her pale, fat thighs at us.

I only remember her clapping her hands loudly once. My next memory is of the faces of the Corsican goons spitting on us as we lay sprawled on the steps. Both our purses were gone. You must have staggered away to your cold, smelly bed in the library of your house on the Tiber. Since you no longer had your purse, you couldn't have gone to any of your other shady hideouts. You must have, of course, sung those boring old love songs on the way. I somehow managed to get into my tent in the camp without letting the guards discover my condition.

It was while I was having myself massaged the next morning, that the messenger arrived. My head still reeling, I read the Commander's order: Move the battalion to Britain. Today! I uprooted myself from Rome that day, Antonius. And the places Augustus and then Tiberius have whirled me through since then! Carthage, Cordoba, Smyrna, Armenia, Damascus, Alexandria! And now this is my seventh year in this parched country of the Jews.

Edo, Antonius, you mustn't be jealous of me for what I am about to tell you. Think of the many breeds of honeyed lips I have kissed! The array of fabulous wines that have tormented my nerves! The battlefields I have watched flowing with blood. The death sentences my pen has scribbled! I have breathed strange winds, known bewitching flowers and wondrous trees, had as pets fabulous birds and great dogs. But ask me, Antonius, if I feel satisfied when I look back, and I have no answer. I did my duty by my Emperor and for the Empire. And I enjoyed all the pleasures that came along with that. That's all. This is the lot in life that Father Jupiter (I will not strike that out, old chap, it is clear I have begun to think of God) has assigned me. Who am I to decide whether it is right or wrong?

Once, in the midst of my wanderings and my journeys up life's ladders, I tried to get news of you and it was then that I learned that you had sold your mansion and the Persian carpet shop on the floor beneath, given away your collection of books to the Marcus Longinus school, and disappeared. Then I remembered your dreams of adventure and thought you must have set sail for Hindustan or China.

If only you'd paid the slightest attention to my words, Antonius, none of this would have been necessary. Didn't I always tell you that a man must marry at a certain stage of his life? Was it because there was no woman wealthy or beautiful enough for you in the city of Rome that you lived all by yourself, like a worm, amidst those dusty books? A good woman would have mellowed your endless lust and passions into a homely flame. Instead you chose Nubian eunuchs who tore your flesh with their nails, pretty Armenian boys who kissed you with dry lips, Roman prostitutes who gave you cruel satisfaction. Fate, Antonius, simple fate.

But I found myself a suitable Roman girl who gave my exile a foundation of comfort. Julia was a student at Longinus's school. Like you, she too collects books. Her thoughts, like yours, are wild and wandering. Why are we born? Why do we have relationships? What happens after death? What is truth? Is there only one truth? And now, I leave Julia alone and so does she, me. Thank heavens! If nothing else, she has put up with my snoring all these years. Isn't that enough?

Which does not mean, Antonius, that I live in respectable piety. Tell me, is there anything a Roman governor might not do? And do my desires have limits? I love wine, women, food, soft beds, fast horses, and the company of birds and animals. What can I do? History has cast all this bait my way. I nibble at each in turn and wait. The day will come when I swallow the bait and history's fishing rod casts me ashore. *Dhum*! Some thrashing about and it will all be over. History will no longer have any use for me. The rod will go down again for the next catch. And so it goes.

It is as if our old days and Rome itself are fading from my mind. Only the flavour of Roman wine stays with me. The bodiless wines of these Jews are not fit even to be sampled. But the Jewesses – they're another matter altogether. What stunners they are, Antonius! All their prudery and modesty, their prayers and fasts, is like a smokescreen. Once we grope our way through and trap them within the four edges of a bed, what single-mindedness! Their supple bodies are a far cry from the fat indolence of Roman women. I suspect the Jewish men are totally useless. In our days you and I could have run riot here! But what's the use of thinking that now? That's life. You can only have either this or that. If the wine is bad in one place the women are good. And in another place the wine is good but the women are not satisfactory. There are places where the wine, women, fish and fruit are all equally good. But then we are not there.

Antonius! If you can somehow bring yourself here after you get this letter, I can put all this your way. But going by your letter, your affairs seem to be in a mess. What is this *refuge* you claim to be running in the outskirts of Rome? What are you up to – improving the Roman Empire and the world? What is your aim in rehabilitating a handful of prostitutes and in giving destitute women a shelter to bear their children and taking charge of the babies? And you provide grazing lands for decrepit horses turned loose to die and persuade street villains, whose services we used to buy with the flash of a coin, to work in your farm! Tell you what, go and reform the Emperor and the senators instead, if you can. Look, can you really save the Roman Empire by improving the lot of fifty people or even five hundred? Isn't that up to the Emperors? Isn't it they who possess the authority, the might, the armies, the tax collectors? When they build highways, construct a coliseum, raise temples, dig wells and stage plays, history is made. And it has its brief high points when war breaks out and conquests are made. Where is the room for salvation in all this? And who is to save whom? What's your place in this? I at least have the role of a tool.

And let me tell you, even if you try to save someone it doesn't work. I haven't yet told you about that. But that is the fact. That is what history is all about. There will always be soldiers and whores and street boys. And animals abandoned to die. On the other side there will be emperors, aristocrats, senators and people like you, who spend their lives in libraries. The sun rises. Night falls. There's cold, heat, childhood, youth, old age, death. Sometimes it rains and sometimes not. Some olives taste good, others do not. Some wells are always full, others run dry halfway through summer. Antonius, history shows no mercy. Have no faith in saviours who appear as part of history, for they too have swallowed the bait of history. If it is a woman that destroys a man like me in the end, what brings about the downfall of saviours is some idea that traps them worse than a woman's hold. Finally, one day, it's just one tug on the rod. *Dhum!* The tail flicks twice, the mouth gapes, the gills flare. Finished! And so Antonius, my dear friend, give up this futile work of yours, get back, find yourself a good woman (leave that to me, ha!), build a comfortable house on the Tiber or in the quiet of the Appian Way, buy more books if you want to, and begin to live the rest of your life happily.

Of course, you must have children too. Not having children robs you of something. The wife and the servants will bring them up, don't worry. We don't have to break our heads over them. It doesn't even matter that we shall see them only rarely. But they should be in place. Otherwise, we will die with a sense of not having left anything tangible behind. But children are a gamble, Antonius. Suppose you have children who become brave warriors or renowned figures. Just imagine basking in the sun, seated in the veranda of a huge villa in the empire they build. Wouldn't that be a great pleasure? But it is certain that the greater the authority, strength and wealth we bestow upon our children, the more they will rise against us, and stake their claims at the point of a sword. It may be that they will kill us or that we will have to kill them. Or it may be that history will kill them, as happened with the young fellow I tried to save some days ago. But it does not matter. That is what this game called history is all about. If Jupiter intervenes in our favour in this game, we are lucky (see how circumspect I am).

I don't mean to dismiss your *refuge* contemptuously. In fact, if your letter had come two weeks earlier, I would have found some way to rescue that young man Yeshu from those Jews, and sent him to your shelter. He would have fitted in with your strange ways of thinking. Perhaps even with your old lifestyle! For it was mostly beautiful Jewesses who waited for him at the trial with tears flowing down their cheeks. (Let me add that there were one or two that I knew among them.)

You must therefore understand that I am not discouraging you. Look, who but you and I must show historical responsibility towards Roman whores, criminals and horses! Perhaps that young fellow I couldn't save from death would have partnered your effort to save people. Perhaps the two of you together might have managed to save the Roman Empire, or even the whole world. (From what? From whom? I don't know.) And when I die and go to the world of the dead, I, who helped you, could have claimed a golden throne to the right of Jupiter and all kinds of bliss!

What fine dreams! I have only one question, Antonius. What sort of a saviour is a fellow who can't even save himself? Wasn't it a mere stab that felled Julius Caesar, who was the hero and saviour of the whole world? A saviour must fulfil certain conditions. He must have a blueprint on how to solve the problems of not only the Roman Empire but this whole world, and create a perfect abode of bliss – all instantaneously. He must have the strength to delight in all this and not to die, to continue to live and savour the wonderful status of a saviour. He must ensure that he has the political authority or the military backing or the magical powers necessary to achieve this end. He can't be a saviour one minute and need saving himself the next. That would be deceiving those who gather around him – and himself.

I wish you'd been with me when I interrogated this fellow Yeshu. You would probably have understood the incoherent things he said. To be honest, I didn't understand any of it. If you'd been there, I think you might have told me how to extricate the poor chap from the hands of those treacherous Jews. I'm sure you know I've sentenced to death countless men, women and children. I have no special feelings about that. I performed those tasks for my Emperor and my Empire, that is all. But when I turned over that young Jew to those rascally priests, for them to thrash and kill, I felt a little distressed. But he had brought the situation on himself. Because he just wasn't there. He was in a dream. And he didn't even have the primary sense of survival in the midst of mortal danger.

He was perhaps the first person in my life I tried to *save*. I wish he had realized that as well. How far from the code can a Justice of the Roman Empire stray? Let me tell you that what I felt for him was not pity. I don't think he would have accepted pity. There was something in him I could identify but not touch. It lay like a shadow behind the veil of thought and the look of weariness on his face. An elusive something I couldn't quite measure, slippery as a fish. An obstinate way of staying out of reach, no matter how far you extended your hand. At the same time, there was a kind of affection in his stance, his look, his movements. Even when he was being whipped, a whiff of love seemed to waft from him, sweetly, as from an attar tree in bloom. The way I understood it, he was neither a rebel nor a liar but an innocent man in search of a dream, and even in the thick of danger, he was in the grip of that dream.

You're going to say that he reminded me of some pretty boy I once knew. No, it's not that, Antonius. Truly, it isn't. Can't you give me the benefit of the doubt at least sometimes? I don't care if you taunt me, but what I felt then was an urge to hold him to my chest like a kitten or a puppy, to fondle him and take care of him. Or to hold him in the hollow of my palm like a nestling and stroke him. But I was sure he would bite or scratch or peck at me even as I fondled him. Because, behind that love, he was holding fast to some mysterious thing.

You know, Antonius, someone told me he was a magician. It must have been some such hidden power that drove and dragged him to his death. Whatever it was, this fellow who went about saying that he was the saviour of the Jews had to finally take leave of them hanging limp and broken on a wooden cross, like a piece of mistletoe. Neither he nor the Jews were saved. The reason for my telling you all this is to beseech you not to push your saving mission to such an extent. What's the use of second thoughts after you're dead? Who will care if you go up a cross tomorrow, suffer a great deal of pain and breathe your last? All you will earn is a bad reputation. If you were young and handsome and famous, you'd at least be posthumously adored by some beauties, right?

I'll tell you something funny. When I was interrogating him, I stole a glance at the group of women watching him from one side. You know ... after all, judges too should have an eye for beauty! And who do I see but my own girl, the uncrowned queen of Jewish pleasure-girls, Magdalena Mariam herself, tears flowing down her cheeks! How many nights had I made her jump the wall into my garden pavilion, and scale the heights of ecstasy under the stars! Even jumping the wall was a kind of foreplay for her! For many days I had not seen or heard of her and I'd been looking for her.

And there she was, looking at me like a sacred virgin, with red, tear stained eyes. I started in astonishment. It was just luck that I did not show any sign of recognition from the seat of justice. When I looked again, I realized that her eyes were registering a mute appeal to me. I understood. She too had been chasing after this fellow, Yeshu. She was pleading for his life! I thought to myself: Edo Yeshu, this is quite something! I have lost an expert in garden follies because of you! I could condemn you to death just for this offence! But I will not do that. Because you are essentially harmless. These women run after you because they are silly. I realize all this. I forgive you.

Just as I was thinking this, Julia's maid came running with a message from her mistress. Would you believe it? (I know you will, you too deal in dreams and strange sciences.) Julia had written: Please do not harm this good man, I dreamed of him the other night. Here was Julia saying exactly what I was thinking. And she was saying she had known it through a dream! Aha, Yeshu! I looked at him in astonishment. You charmed not only Jewesses, but my Roman wife as well, and that through a dream, is it? Yeshu stood there, looking at me. Suddenly he turned, quick as an eel, as if he had suddenly had an idea, and looked behind him, towards where Magdalena Mariam and the others stood. I looked at Mariam too. I saw her eyes widen and her face, wet with tears, blaze as if it had been struck by lightning. I felt envious. I had showered potfuls of gold upon her and heaped sweet endearments. But she had never looked at me like that, not even once. Her face had never glowed like that for me. In one sense, Antonius, who knows what these women really want?

I still have news to tell you. Tomorrow my sugar-girl, my secretary, will come. I'll write the rest then. Since she is just a girl – and Julia's friend as well – I will not be able to write so frankly. I shall now lock up what I have written. You can't trust these women. How can we let beautiful, good natured Ruth into our secrets – what will she think of us! She'll of course think we are a couple of dirty old Romans! Ha! Wouldn't that reflect badly on the great Roman Empire and Emperor Tiberius, lord and master of his subjects? Ah, how difficult it is to live as a decent Roman citizen!

THE SECRETARY DISCOVERS CERTAIN MISTAKES

Ruth (twenty three years), secretary to Pontius Pilate, Roman Governor of the Province of Judaea, sits behind her desk in the garden pavilion of the Governor's residence in Jerusalem, awaiting Pilate's arrival. It is ten o'clock in the morning. The Roman pillars and statues in the garden are basking in the sun. A dry wind blows in from the Red Sea. Signs of the night's drizzle can be seen on the ground. The sunlight carries the scent of rain. A white cat rubs itself against one of the pillars of the pavilion, looks at Ruth and mews loudly as if demanding something. Ruth puts it on her lap and strokes it.

Ruth (to the cat): You're a Roman cat, aren't you? Never

satisfied, no matter how much you get. Wretch! She bends down to kiss it. The cat notices an insect on a flowering plant and springs towards it.

Ruth (to the cat): Out! Out you go! Go and fetch your master!

The cat comes back, having failed to catch what it had run after. It sits at Ruth's feet, looks at her with its blue and gold eyes and mews plaintively again.

Ruth (to the cat, raising her leg as if to kick it): Chi, ungrateful creature! Off with you!

She looks at the cat with feigned anger. The luscious leg that darted out from beneath Ruth's blue robe into the sunlight to threaten the cat, brightens up the pavilion momentarily. The cat curls up under Ruth's writing table and closes its eyes.

Ruth is lost in thought as she looks at the city of Jerusalem, visible on the horizon beyond the garden walls. She is a short, sweetly rounded yet perfectly shaped beauty. Her curly hair falls in waves over her shoulders and back. The leg which darted out earlier like a flash of lightning is now crossed over the other under the blue robe. The blue veins that run under the sandals on her pink and white feet dissolve into the henna of her toenails. Even when lost in thought, her face glows with brightness. Her lips, which suggest obstinacy, quiver on the edge of a smile. The same smile hides in the corner of her eyes. There is a faint touch of arrogance on her face.

Ruth (to herself): What has happened today? The old man

hasn't come out yet. He must have had one drink too many last night. The cat has arrived. Now the dog will follow, then the parrot, the ostrich, the baby deer, the elephant and the rabbit. And trailing behind them, Governor Pontius Pilate, swaying and tottering. That is, if he can hold his head up this morning. It is such a relief to know that the old man cares at least for these animals.

In the letter he wrote to some old friend and hid in his box yesterday, he says he loves me like a daughter! Like a daughter! Only a stupid Roman girl would believe that. Am I to think that when his foot comes out under the desk while I am taking dictation and brushes against mine, he is only stretching his limbs? All right, I'll believe that. But there is certainly something not quite right about the way he peeps over my shoulders, touching and yet not touching, to look at what I've written. Woman that I am, I think there is something there. Still, I'll give the old man the benefit of the doubt.

In one sense, this Pilate is a harmless creature. He has absolutely no idea of what is happening in the world. Once he gets up in the morning, he is in a world of his own. Life, for him, is what he sees in front of his nose. If he sees a girl, he stares at her. If he sees an animal, he goes up to it and fondles it. Occasionally the animal, on its part, kicks or bites or butts him. If it shows him just a little affection, he will sit with it for hours on end. If a woman shows him affection, he gets confused.

After that, everything is handled by those thieving servants. Only Jehovah knows how he manages to govern the province of Judaea. It is thanks to the sheer inefficiency of the Roman Empire that his job and the governance of this land go on somehow.

Locking things up is a habit of his. He thinks that no one sees or looks for what he locks up. The old man does not realize the logic of this world, that the first thing people who look for secrets do is to open locks. When I think of all this, I sometimes long to catch hold of that Roman nose, tweak it and caress the old man. What is there in that big ivory box that Julia and I have not seen? But he keeps writing foolish things and putting them away inside it. He has love letters and even love poems. And the thrilling secrets of the great Roman Empire, including those of the Emperor's sexual disasters and their peculiar remedies, that have come out of that box and lodged themselves in this head of mine!

Julia and I know the name of every lover of his, male or female. The way Julia puts it is: As long as Pilate doesn't give me any trouble, I don't want to know any of this. I've forgiven him long back. True enough, he does not bother Julia at all. All that is over. Moreover, he is afraid of her. He has a feeling that she knows a lot more than he does. He is afraid of the books she reads and of her meditations. He shudders, thinking that they are all traps. I have seen his hand tremble as if he were holding ice blocks when he secretly takes out Julia's books and goes through them. I have also seen him enter her meditation room and then rush out, sweating profusely, rolling his eyes, as if he had seen a ghost. My dear Pilate, when you finally learn that your wife Julia worships the feet of that Yeshu whom you handed over to be killed, how much more you will perspire, how much rounder your eyes will grow!

You wrote to Antonius that you think Yeshu entered Julia's dream by some kind of sorcery! How many times your beautiful and sweet natured wife has come with me, old Pilate, unknown to you, her face veiled, to sit at our beloved Yeshu's feet! You made Mariam jump the wall, Governor, and I made your wife jump the wall as well. Would you really have known if your wife had jumped the wall for another man? No. For you live in a self-created muddle of a dream world. Truth to tell, that is why I have a kind of affection for you. There is a kind of unpreparedness in your life filled with lust. And just as you do not love anyone, you bear no malice towards anyone either, I think. But what's the use? The simpleton within you carries out evil work too, with equal dispassion.

And as for your boasts, we forgave those long ago. The things you have claimed in the letter to that old boozing and fornicating companion! Reading it, one would imagine that Pilate is the cupid of Jerusalem. But Mariam, Rahel and Anna have all told me stories of their encounters with you. All you manage is some grappling and tumbling, some heavy breathing and looking on. Listen, Pilate, if these are the peaks of ecstasy you describe to your companion, you're welcome to them. But Mariam says that you leave her behind at ground zero when you scale those heights.

And then you feel sad, don't you, because she does not look at you with a glowing face? And because she looked at Yeshu like that! How will you ever understand that a single look of our friend bestows the bliss of a thousand passions put together? Well, if you'd been the kind of man who could understand that, you wouldn't have needed to call for a vessel of water to wash your hands that sad morning.

How can we ever make you understand that the joy Yeshu gave us was not what you think? It was not our lips or breasts that Yeshu kissed. It was not through the passage between our thighs that he entered us. It was our hearts that he kissed like the breeze on a rose. It was our souls he entered, breaking through our allurements. But does that mean that we haven't coveted his embraces? Don't we yearn for them still? We do! On one occasion he suddenly placed his hand on my shoulder. Oh, the flash of fire that coursed through this body of mine that no man has ever entered! The insides of my thighs were wet. My breasts sprang up lovingly. But when I looked into his eyes, I found myself leaving my body and flying like a bird into a bright sphere. If only he had touched us over and again! And embraced us! And slept with us, dreamt with us, snuggled under a blanket with us, and fallen prey to our secret scents! But his heart was in another world. A world we could sometimes glimpse but never enter.

Pilate, you only saw Mariam and Martha and the other women weep. You never saw Julia and me cry for him, did you? We too have shed tears for him as for a lover. We stayed awake for Yeshu on the night of his capture while you drank and gorged with that vile one eyed general from Damascus past midnight and then lay snoring. But now we have no more grief. We have not wept for him since that day.

Do you know that he has risen from the dead? No. Do you know that he will soon come to see us? No. Pilate, what do you know? Why should we be afraid now? Why should we grieve? We wept at his helplessness that day. We saw his fatigue and wept. We saw his blood and wept. You had him flogged. It was a body already broken by the blows of the priests that you had whipped again.

We are prepared to believe a part of what you told Julia, that you did that to save him. Sometimes, even evil men stumble into good deeds! But, was it not the message that Julia and I sent, that made you change your mind? But for that, would you have changed your role and tried to become Yeshu's saviour? Would you have boasted of your sense of justice? The things you have said in that letter! That you tried to save Yeshu and that he refused! That he was a victim of history and a powerless messiah! Pilate, I, who love Yeshu, say that not even God, his father, would have been able to save him. Who knows him as well as we do, the women who are his friends?

Pilate, shall I tell you the biggest failure of Yeshu, whom you did not understand? It was that he did not open all the doors of his world to us women and invite us to enter. He wasted his time with those donkeys, whom he called disciples. Had he given us the time, the attention and the patience he gave them, perhaps he would not have had to do what he had to do, so soon and so frighteningly! He kept his mother at a distance. And his sisters too. Who can protect a man's soul the way a mother, a wife, a lover or a sister can? If only he had held on to his mother in the hurly-burly of seeking his father! Instead, he got lost in the dark alleys of paternity. What did it matter who his father was? Is not the womb the real father? What a pity! Who will change his mind? Will the resurrected man go back, fall at poor Mariam's feet and say, Mother, I recognize you? This time, I will ask him to his face to do that.

But how do I first get him out of the earshot of those cunning disciples? Now that he is resurrected, they will cling to him all the more – and run away from him just as fast when it comes to the crunch. Pilate, my boss, it was that bunch of scoundrels that you should have had thrashed good and proper. Someone said that when the priests caught hold of Yeshu in the Garden of Gethsemane, one of the disciples ran away dropping even his clothes! Oh my Yeshu, that you should have come to such a pass! If it is this way today, what will be the state of your Kingdom of God in future? Why did you not share with us your secrets? Why did you not ask us to that final supper? Wouldn't we have at least helped you serve the food? How did you have the heart to entrust the burden of your Kingdom of God to a group of men who have no spirit or character? Wouldn't we have gathered your Kingdom of God into our very wombs? Wouldn't we have nurtured it and spread it over heaven and earth? I fear that something even more terrible is going to happen to you because you spurned our love, and your mother. Had you possessed us like a man, Yeshu, you would never have dreamed up a Kingdom of God with no place for womanhood. Why did you alienate your Kingdom from our love, the support and shelter only we can give? That was your great loss. And ours. Let it be. What is lost, is lost.

(Ruth heaves a deep sigh.) I am frightened, Yeshu. If you have risen from the dead, what will you be like, having come back from death? You must have become even more of a stranger, more wary, more distant. I am reluctant to see you again. What if you have become a mere form without body, breath, scent or warmth? Will I be able to touch that hand again, the hand through which lightning courses?

(Ruth sighs again and bends forward covering her face with

her hands. After a while, she raises her head suddenly.) Ah, there he comes, at last, the Governor of all Judaea! What does he have as companion today? A baby mule! Fit company!

Ruth (looks under the table, prods the cat and says): Edi, get up! Here comes your master. Run up to him and wind yourself around his feet. He'll be happy.

Ruth (to herself): Let Pilate come to check my handwriting today! He should improve his own writing and language first. The letter he wrote to Antonius is full of mistakes. Shame on him! If he comes and tries to stand behind me today, I'll give him a push. Let him realize how hard the floor of the pavilion can be without Mariam to cushion him. Or, no, let him be. When he stands bashfully in front of me, mere speck that I am, I feel sorry for him.

Ruth gets up and bows to Pilate: Why are you so late, sir? You overslept, didn't you? Where did you get this new mule? From Syria? Did you have to bring a mule from so far away, sir? It's a special breed, is it? I don't know anything about mules, sir. What is there to write today, sir? No, sir, I'm not fed up with waiting. It's so pleasant to sit here, sir, isn't it? I sat thinking of many things. Oh, nothing in particular. I was thinking about that Yeshu who died on the cross the other day. Were you too thinking of him, sir? How amazing, sir! He was a gentle person, wasn't he, sir? You were not able to do anything for him, sir. To whom is the letter, sir? To Antonius?

That's a new name, sir. So, he's an old friend of yours, sir.
That's good. It's an occasion for you, sir, to renew memories.
The cat was waiting to get on to your lap, sir. She's happy now.
Shall we start then, sir? Be careful, sir. That baby mule is
eating the hem of your robe!

PILATE CONTINUES HIS LETTER

The pavilion in Pilate's garden. Pilate is reclining on a heavy throne. The cat is curled up on his lap. He strokes it with one hand. Although Ruth sees the baby mule wreaking havoc upon the plants on the other side, she pretends that she does not. Ruth waits with her pen.

Pilate (with a deep sigh): Let's begin, then. (Silently) What can I write with her sitting here? All right. Anyway ... (to Ruth) The letter is to my friend Titus Antonius in Rome. There's no need for the seal and all that. Just start straight off.

Ruth (to Pilate): Why, sir?

Pilate (uneasily): It's all right. He's my friend.

Ruth (to Pilate): Yes, sir.

Pilate: My dear Antonius, this is to continue with the news I wrote you earlier.

Ruth (to Pilate): When did you write, sir?

Pilate (with increasing unease): Oh, I wrote that myself.

Ruth (to Pilate): Did you send the letter, sir? I don't seem to remember sending it, sir.

Pilate (swallowing his anger): You did not come that day, child. A messenger came and I sent it off.

Ruth: Oh, all right then, sir. (Silently) Those who speak white lies must also know how to get away with them. You do not even know how to lie convincingly. (To Pilate) And the rest, sir?

Pilate (to Ruth): We'll begin, then. I need to concentrate now. Don't interrupt me with questions, child. It will distract the flow of my thought.

Ruth (to Pilate): If I don't hear properly, I can clear doubts, can't I, sir?

Pilate (with a deep sigh): All right. (Silently) If only she would stretch her leg out a little. It's a pretty leg. But like all Jewesses, she keeps it covered, under control and out of sight. What does one do? (To Ruth) Start writing.

Ruth (silently): Here comes the great flow of thought.

Pilate: I will go on with what we were talking about. (A long silence.)

Ruth (to Pilate): Sir?

Pilate (to himself): What can I say with her sitting here? I've often thought she's a little too smart. What shall I do now?

Ruth (to Pilate): What is it, sir? Didn't you sleep well last night? (Silently) He is worried that he will give himself away. It looks as if I'll be let off today.

Pilate (to Ruth): Look child, didn't Julia say she wanted to go somewhere today? You can go with her. I'll stay here and scribble a few things.

Ruth (silently): Don't forget to lock it up. Because we want to read the rest of the story this evening, when we come back after meeting the resurrected Yeshu. (To Pilate) All right, sir. May I leave then, sir?

Pilate nods.

Ruth (silently): Let's play a game with the old man now.

Under the pretence of tying the strap of her sandal, Ruth casually lifts the edge of her robe and exhibits the noteworthy, pretty leg she had exposed a little while ago.

Ruth (bending down, silently): Just one look only, Pilate, just one glance. Even my Yeshu has not seen this.

Pilate starts and the cat wakes up. Confusion, astonishment and breathlessness are registered on Pilate's face. He looks around furtively. Holding on to both sides of the throne tightly, he sits like a statue, staring at Ruth. Ruth slowly straightens up. He looks as if he has been dealt a stunning blow.

Ruth (to Pilate): They're poor quality sandals, sir.

Pilate gives another start.

Pilate: Yes, yes.

Ruth (smiling sweetly at Pilate): I'm sure your hand will ache, sir, after all the writing you're going to do. Don't you want me to help you at all, sir?

Pilate: What? Yes, yes ... No, no.

Ruth climbs down from the pavilion and bows to Pilate. Pilate returns the greeting with a hand that is still trembling from the sudden start. Ruth drives away the baby mule, which is eating the flowering plants. Then she walks slowly towards the house. The cat runs after her, its tail raised, mewing as it runs.

Ruth (silently): You wrote, didn't you, to your friend, that the modesty of Jewish girls is false? Now you can write more in that strain.

Pilate sits for a long time staring in front of him like a blind man. He finally picks up his pen and begins to write.

Edo Antonius! I tried to dictate the rest of the letter to my secretary, failed, and am writing this now myself. Although the dictation was not successful, something amazing, incredible and beautiful happened today. Long live cobblers who make bad sandals! I cannot tell you here all that happened. But I must say that my faith in Jupiter grows steadily when such blessings are showered on me.

Antonius, I don't know why, a certain uneasiness lingers in me when I think of Yeshu, the young man they crucified. And now I hear a rumour that he has been resurrected. This creates a problem. Not that I am afraid. If that youth rises up from the dead and comes walking towards me, I will only be delighted to meet him. If he and you agree, I can even send him to you! Yes? Ha! If this Yeshu comes back and becomes the King and Saviour of the Jews, I am quite sure he will have the honesty to acknowledge what I tried to do for him! He will certainly not send me to the gallows!

That isn't what worries me, Antonius. What if he becomes a messiah, establishes a generation of disciples, spreads his message throughout the world, is transformed into a great being and sustains his reputation and his fame over a thousand or two thousand years? What makes me think this way is his peculiar confidence. In my opinion, it's a sign of something that could last for a long time to come. What would be my place in the chronicles of that kingdom? Don't we have to be a little careful then? What have we to lose if we can have a good name two thousand years hence? In any case, I want to tell you at least about these things, in order to clear my mind. This is what happened, Antonius.

The Jewish elders and their attendants had tied him up and brought him to my palace. The sun was yet to rise and I had indulged in some drinking and revelling the night before. Just as I had laid down and shut my eyes the servant knocked and called me. Somehow supporting my heavy head, I managed to put on my clothes and come out. And there was this crowd, and this man Yeshu. Day was just breaking in the east. I took one look and went in again. I went into the bath and poured cold water over my head. I put a finger down my throat and tried to throw up. I sat on the toilet for a long time. Then I went back and sat down on the seat of justice, feeling rotten, like a man about to die. I could not even keep my eyes open. Yeshu kept fading away before them. A servant who realized my plight brought me a potion in a jug. A wonder drink made by mixing Roman wine and herbs from Hindustan. It revived me somewhat.

I asked the man one chief question: Are you the King of Jews? The accusation they had brought against him was that he had gone around saying that he was. The reply Yeshu gave me was a retort that deserved a slap in his face, That is what you say. But I forgave him that. Then he added that his kingdom was not of this world. There ended the problem. Why should the Roman Empire bother about a kingdom that was not of this world? He also said he had been born in order to be a witness to the truth. Nothing wrong with that either? But I asked, out of curiousity: What is truth? Can you tell me? For, he spoke of truth so easily.

Then I went out and said to the Jews: I do not think this

man has done anything wrong. Today is the feast of the Passover. You know that it is customary to free a prisoner on this day. Let it be this man. But the Jews shouted that it was Barabbas the thief they wanted to be freed. Crucify Yeshu, they yelled.

The strength of the potion had begun to wane. I signalled for another jugful. Then I went to the bathroom and cooled my head again. As I swallowed the second jug, I had an idea. If I punished Yeshu in front of everyone, the matter would perhaps end. I had Yeshu scourged with a whip. And someone placed a crown of thorns on his head – a little joke. I snatched the opportunity to close my eyes for a little while, resting my head on my hands.

I woke up when I heard a great commotion. The Jews would settle for nothing less than Yeshu's life. It was at this moment that I noticed Mariam standing at a distance, and also received Julia's message. I was in big trouble. I went up to Yeshu and asked him: Young man, where are you actually from? Are you from this world? Silence. Then I said to him: Do you understand that I have the authority to set you free and also the power to crucify you? Why don't you talk to me? He answered this too with a foolish retort. Still, I was not angry. Because I could see that he was a truthful fellow who had fallen into a trap of his own making. But as I said in the beginning, Antonius, you can save only those who want to be saved.

The crowd was growing increasingly restless. The situation was taking a serious turn. People were talking politics! Voices rose, proclaiming allegiance to the Emperor and decrying me. Everything in me that understood public life cried out, Danger, danger! I made a final effort to save Yeshu for Julia's sake. I sent him to Herod, the King of the Jews, for his verdict. Herod was in Jerusalem just then on some nefarious mission. I had heard that he had a fad for magicians and astrologers. That I detest him is another matter. If he, as King of the Jews, let Yeshu go free, the priests would be forced to keep their mouths shut. But that stupid man, Herod, sent Yeshu back to me without taking any action. I learnt later that Yeshu did not answer his questions either. The only good was that I gained a little time to have a short nap.

What could I do after that? The crowd was becoming unruly. I looked at Yeshu. He stood looking at me, his face still giving out love. I then sent for a vessel of water. Washing my hands for all to see, I cried out: I take no part in shedding the blood of this just man. You can do whatever you want with him. I looked at Yeshu once more. Nothing had changed on that tired face. I turned him over to the Jews. Need I describe the melee and manhandling soldiers and mobs indulge in, once a man is handed over to be crucified? Everything that followed was terrible, as usual.

I sometimes wonder whether Ruth too has fallen into Yeshu's

snare. She's a Jewess after all. And a good looking one. Sometimes I have felt that Julia's friends are not politically reliable. But – peace in the family is what is most important, my Antonius. And you of course know that sinners like us cannot raise our voices too high to accuse others. Silence is wisest. Time will provide an answer to everything.

Will Yeshu come to see me, if he has risen from the dead? What do you think? Then again, why should he ? His kingdom is somewhere else. Of course, being an administrator, I have a curiosity of a historical nature as to whether he will actually establish his Kingdom of God some day. If that promises to be a good place, Antonius, both of us must undergo a change of heart – you have already done so, haven't you? – and lead a cosy life there. Let this letter of mine go on record as standing application for that. Keep it safely. Shelter it among your books. What position would you like to hold in Yeshu's Kingdom? You can be the librarian. I will manage the zoo – and the harem! Do you think we'll be fed up after a while? Let's see, let's try it out. I'll be waiting for your reply. May all good things come to you.

Your sincere friend,

Pontius Pilate

THE SECRETARY BECOMES UNCONSCIOUS

A path winds its way out of Jerusalem over barren hills and valleys, and through parched plateaus that have been taken over by stones and shrubs. It is clear that this country road, which has never borne the marks of cartwheels or horses' hooves, belongs exclusively to goatherds, to women who come to gather kindling for fire, and to travellers from remote villages going this way to worship at the great temple at Jerusalem. This road had not been made for anyone who wants to go anywhere in a hurry. It had taken shape gradually over the years on this patch of earth, under the feet of the nameless and the homeless, travelling to bring about the humblest and most anonymous events of history. It does not look very different from the dust on either side of it – except that it is a little firmer. The only signs of life upon it are weathered animal droppings. There are no sights to catch your attention even in the distance. Lifeless hills and stretches of flat land, which fade into the sunlight. Travellers who wish to see something less harsh must raise their heads and look up at the sky, where clouds may be seen trapped in a wind or the gleam of the blue sky or, rarely, a few birds. And, of course, the sun. If it is night, they can glimpse the flickering course of the Milky Way. He who catches sight of a scorpion that has been startled by his footfall on the gravel is truly fortunate. And those who see a fleeing fox or a prowling rabbit, have had an unforgettable day.

It is on this path now (that is, at this moment, when Pontius Pilate has finished his letter to Titus Antonius, closed and sealed it and put it aside for a messenger to take, eaten lunch and is resting) that Pilate's wife, Julia, secretary Ruth, their friends Magdalena Mariam, Martha and two or three other women are walking. Julia is in Jewish dress and has a veil over her face. The women's voices rise and fail as they walk. Sometimes one talks to another, but most of the time one addresses all the others. As the discussion grows heated, their pace slows down. The subjects they discuss vary and branch off one from the other.

Ruth (looking up at the sky): I think it's going to rain.

The others look up at the sky casually, as they walk.

Mariam: Oh, no, those are not rain clouds. It doesn't look as if it will rain now. It would be good if it did. It's so hot.

A woman (to Mariam): How can you be so sure that Yeshu will come this way?

Mariam: I'm not really sure. I hope he will, that's all. If we don't see him today we'll look for him somewhere else another day. Even if we don't know where he is, shouldn't he know where we are? Let's believe he does.

Ruth: My feet are aching, walking like this. And my sandals are pinching my feet too. It must be a punishment for having taken them off today to play a trick.

Martha: What trick?

Ruth (smiling): I can't tell you. You'd laugh at me.

The group, which had stopped for a while to talk about the rain, moves forward again. Tiny gusts of wind stir up the dust here and there on the path. Clouds gather in the sky as if preparing for rain. But, as Mariam said, they don't appear quite ready as yet to come down as rain. The sun is still bright. A screen of steaming dust trembles at the edge of the rocky desert and over the distant hills. A roar reverberates through the air like the peal of distant thunder. Forks of lightning flash noiselessly through scattered clouds. The wind descends from the sky to the earth. It blows powerfully against the journeying women, pushing their veils away from their heads, making their hair fly back and their robes cling to their bodies.

Julia: What a lovely breeze!

Everyone agrees.

Martha: It's a sure sign of rain. When it's a cold breeze that blows, it's raining somewhere far away.

A woman: I've come away having hung out the clothes to dry.

Martha: Oh! My lambs will be caught in the rain! They were born just yesterday. The mother is tied up in the yard.

Ruth (bending down and looking at her feet): I can't walk another step. Both my feet are sore.

Martha: Ruth, taking dictation and fooling around with friends is not enough. You must do a little physical work sometimes. (To Julia) Can't you make her do some hard work? Sitting with Pilate all the time, she too has acquired a pleasure seeking nature. Excuse me, Julia.

Julia laughs.

The distant rumble heard earlier increases. Clouds have grown still.

Without anyone realizing it, the sun has faded. Suddenly, there is another thunderous sound from the horizon, like an army on the march.

Julia (cries out): Did the earth tremble?

Ruth: Yes. Careful!

The earth trembles as if giant footsteps were approaching. The ground beneath their feet heaves as if a giant animal underneath is in gooseflesh. They stand frozen in the middle of the road, their faces raised to the wind. Screwing up their eyes, they look around fearfully.

Ruth: Ayyo! I have a cramp in my leg.

A woman: No, it's not an earthquake. It must be a landslide or something like that. Don't be afraid.

Another woman: If only it would rain. That would make a difference.

The wind beats down, raising dust. The earth moves again. Someone screams. The sky is completely dark. The women stand motionless on the path, like a group of clay effigies trapped in the wind, gripping each other's hands in fear and looking around them apprehensively. Sheets of whirling dust flies everywhere. And the wind shrieks.

In the distance, through the screen of dust, the figure of a traveller approaching from the opposite direction can be seen indistinctly.

Julia: Someone is coming!

A woman: What a relief. We'll have a man to help us now.

Ruth: Man or woman, all will perish if there's an earthquake.

With difficulty, they pull their veils back on their heads in the teeth of the wind, and stand watching the traveller walk towards them. A roar rises from the horizon filling their ears.

They see that the traveller is barefoot. His face is covered with one end of his headwear. He comes nearer. The women watch him intently. As he approaches, bloodstains are visible on his filthy robe. Hisses of fear and shock arise from them in unison. The newcomer removes the cloth from his face, and throws it across his neck and on to his shoulder. The powerful wind pushes him from behind. A smile spreads over his face, covered with gashes.

Julia: My Yeshu!

Ruth: Aah! (falls to one side, unconscious).

Julia and Martha, drained of all strength, collapse on the ground. Mariam gazes steadily at Yeshu. A smile blossoms slowly on her face. The other women stumble back, shutting with their palms mouths opened to scream.

Mariam moves forward and stands directly in front of Yeshu. She looks closely at his face.

Mariam: This is really you! Was there no one in your father's house to wash your robe?

Mariam takes Yeshu's hands in her own. Yeshu leans forward and kisses her on the cheek. Ruth opens her eyes. She stares at Yeshu without getting up. Yeshu comes up to her, sits down beside her, smiling.

Ruth: Yeshu, you are still a body, aren't you? It's all right, then.

Yeshu takes her right hand in both his hands and kisses

the fingertips. Ruth falls unconscious again. Yeshu removes her sandals, which are tight on her feet, and gently strokes the bruised, reddened feet. The earth quakes again. Yeshu raises his face to the sky and smiles.

LET US READ A FEW APPENDICES

1.   *A note written by Herod, King of Judaea, to Pontius Pilate,*
Roman Governor of Judaea.

Greetings!

So, what news, respected Pilate?

Must we live like this, as strangers to each other? After you contacted me unexpectedly a short while ago, I have been thinking. Am I an enemy of the Roman Empire? No. Do not the Roman Emperor and you respect me? Yes. Then why should there be this distance between the Roman Governor of Judaea and the King of Judaea? Should we not stand together? I am so glad that you thought of me recently. What happened to the magician you sent to me that day? What crime had he committed? I could not make out. Nor could he perform any miracles for me. I had invited my family and friends to watch him perform. Nothing happened.

Please do make a visit to my palace. A heartfelt welcome to you! I will arrange a reception that a great representative of the Roman Empire will find no fault with. I assure you that you will not have cause to be disappointed. Welcome! Welcome!

If you can find the magician, bring him as well. We can enjoy his tricks together, along with many other exclusive things I am going to keep ready for you!

At your service always,

Herod, King of Judaea.

2.   *Monologue of a young man returned from death.*

I hadn't understood all this when I resurrected Lazarus or when I recalled from death the child of Jairus. I said the word and it came to pass, that is all. And now I myself am resurrected! Who uttered the words of life for me? It is all a miracle! Was I in my father's house for two days? I do not remember. Is it that the mother gives us birth, And the father brings us back from the dead? But why does my father elude me? He eluded my mother too. How angry I used to be with her for my not having a father to love! Alas, I should not have done that. It is not a crime for a woman to choose to bear a child from a father the child will never see. She is only receiving into herself the seed of life. The seed of the Kingdom of God. Why didn't I realize all this earlier? Does knowledge always come too late? My mother has already suffered all the agony I caused her. She suffered my death as well. What is the point of my resurrection now? Can my mother's agony be undone? But, even my friends to whom I did not give in, love me still. If that is so, my mother would certainly not have given me up. Why not take Mariam and others along and go see her? Mother will be so happy.

My resurrection will have achieved a little something, then.

3.   *From the letter written by Titus Antonius to Pontius Pilate.*

... All right! When this person Yeshu rises from the dead and comes to you, send him to me! I will take care of him here. I am not a revolutionary like him. But I think I will be able to understand what he says. Together we will try and create a

Kingdom of God! And then we will ask you over. Meanwhile, try to practise some prudence and control and become a better person. It's possible, old chap, it is! Everyone finds a refuge finally – Pilate, even you will receive the benefit of the doubt in the Kingdom of God!

Based on
The Gospel according to St Matthew, Chapters 27, 28
The Gospel according to St Mark, Chapter 15, 16
The Gospel according to St Luke, Chapter 23, 24
The Gospel according to St John, Chapter 18, 19, 20.

Paul Zacharia, educated in Kerala and Karnataka, is one of the best-known writers in Malayalam today. His first collection of short stories was published while he was in his final year at college. Since then five volumes of his short stories, a novella and a collection of essays have been published. He received the Kerala Sahitya Akademi Award for his short stories in 1978. He is currently working on a travelogue through Africa and the Middle East. One of his novellas, *Bhaskara Patelum Ellarum*, has been made into a movie by the renowned film director Adoor Gopalakrishnan. Paul Zacharia has also received the Katha Award for Creative Fiction (1993) and for Translation (1995).

Gita Krishnankutty has been actively involved in translating short stories, novels and anthologies from Malayalam into English. She has a doctorate in English Literature from the University of Mysore. She has received the Katha Award for Translation twice, in 1993 and 2000, and is the recipient of the Crossword Award for Translation (1999).

Indira Chandrasekhar, the editor of this volume, runs a publishing house – Tulika – that publishes books on the social sciences, art and culture, and literary theory. She too is a recipient of the Katha Award for Translation (1997).

OUR RECENT TITLES

THE BEST OF INDIA TRANSLATED.
INDIA TODAY

"A celebration of the Indian experience in all its diversity."
The Express Magazine

VYASA AND VIGHNESHWARA
BY ANAND

"Vyasa and Vighneswara ... interlaces stories within stories, history and fiction, the authentic and the spurious to create a rich and teasing narrative ... this is an accomplished example of the avant garde in Indian vernacular literature."   *The Telegraph*

HAUNTINGS
BANGLA GHOST STORIES
ED BY SUCHITRA SAMANTA

"The stories are wonderful, in that they ... speak of love, loss and longing, of revenge and greed, [and] of life."
Indian Express
2 July, 2000

KATHA PRIZE STORIES 10
ED BY GEETA DHARMARAJAN & NANDITA AGGARWAL

"The tales seem like the uncoding of a secret code ... a journey full of surprises."
The Express Magazine, 21 January, 2001

FORTHCOMING TITLES
KATHA TRAILBLAZER SERIES

Bhupen Khakhar
Two Stories and a Novella
Translated by Ganesh Devy and Naushil Mehta
Gujarati Library/Fiction

Indira Goswami
Pages Stained with Blood
Translated by Pradeep Acharya
Asomiya Library/Fiction

Ashokamitran
Water
Translated by Lakshmi Holmstrom
Tamil Library/Fiction

BE A FRIEND OF KATHA!

If you feel strongly about Indian literature, you belong with us! KathaNet, an invaluable network of our friends, is the mainstay of all our translation-related activities. We are happy to invite you to join this ever-widening circle of translation activists. Katha, with limited financial resources, is propped up by the unqualified enthusiasm and the indispensable support of nearly 5000 dedicated women and men.

We are constantly on the lookout for people who can spare the time to find stories for us, and to translate them. Katha has been able to access mainly the literature of the major Indian languages. Our efforts to locate resource people who could make the lesser-known literatures available to us have not yielded satisfactory results. We are specially eager to find Friends who could introduce us to Bhojpuri, Dogri, Kashmiri, Maithili, Manipuri, Nepali, Rajasthani and Sindhi fiction.

Do write to us with details about yourself, your language skills, the ways in which you can help us, and any material that you already have and feel might be publishable under a Katha programme. All this would be a labour of love, of course! But we do offer a discount of 20% on all our publications to Friends of Katha.

Write to us at –
Katha
A-3 Sarvodaya Enclave
Sri Aurobindo Marg   Call us at: 686-8193, 652-1752
New Delhi   110 017   or E-mail us at: katha@vsnl.com